E
McK

$8.29
McKee, Craig B
The Turned Around Taxi

The TURNED-AROUND TAXI

by Craig B. McKee and Margaret Holland

illustrated by James L. Kersell

THE TURNED-AROUND TAXI is one of a series of Predictable Read Together Books edited by Dr. Margaret Holland. Books in this series are designed to help young children begin to read naturally and easily. See back cover for additional information.

To the turned-around taxicab drivers of Miami

Published by Willowisp Press, Inc., 401 E. Wilson Bridge Road, Worthington, Ohio 43085
Distributed by Sterling Publishing Co., Inc., Two Park Avenue, New York, N.Y. 10016

Library of Congress Catalog Card Number: 85-51102

Printed in the United States of America
10 9 8 7 6 5 4 3 2 1

ISBN 0-87406-033-8

The turned-around taxi, by day or by night,
can never remember his left from his right.

A teacher got into the taxi one day.
"Hurry! Drive to my school. Don't delay."

"Turn right at this corner," the teacher said.
But the turned-around taxi turned left instead.

"Oh, no!" said the teacher. "You've turned the wrong way. You're making me late for school today."

The turned-around taxi, by day or by night,
can never remember his left from his right.

A lawyer got into the taxi one day.
"Hurry! Drive to the court. Don't delay."

"Turn left at this corner," the lawyer said.
But the turned-around taxi turned right instead.

"Oh, no!" said the lawyer. "You've turned the wrong way. You're making me late for court today."

The turned-around taxi, by day or by night,
can never remember his left from his right.

A pilot got into the taxi one day.
"Hurry! Drive to my plane. Don't delay."

"Turn right at this corner," the pilot said.
But the turned-around taxi turned left instead.

"Oh, no!" said the pilot. "You've turned the wrong way. You're making me late for my flight today."

The turned-around taxi, by day or by night,
can never remember his left from his right.

A dancer got into the taxi one day.
"Hurry! Drive to the theater. Don't delay."

"Turn left at this corner," the dancer said.
But the turned-around taxi turned right instead.

"Oh, no!" said the dancer. "You've turned the wrong way. You're making me late for my show today."

The turned-around taxi, by day or by night,
can never remember his left from his right.

Some children got into the taxi one day.
"Please drive to the park. We want to play."

"Turn left at this corner," the children said.
But the taxicab turned off his motor instead.

"I can never remember my left from my right.
I'm all turned around, with no hope in sight."

"Just look at your hands, and stick your thumbs out.
The hand with the 'L' is your LEFT, never doubt."

"Oh, thank you," the taxicab said with delight.
"Now I'll ALWAYS remember my LEFT from my RIGHT."

One piece of confetti, two pieces of confetti, three. . . .